The Gingerbread Man

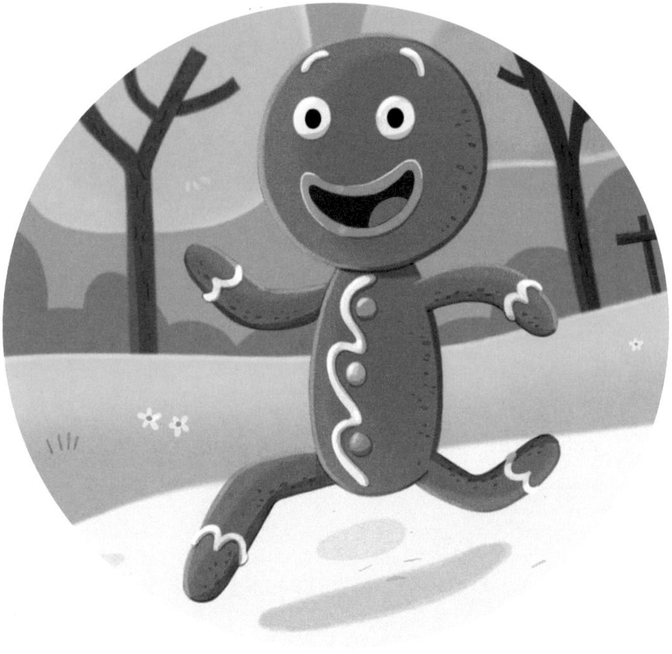

Written by Gill Budgell

Illustrated by Shahab Shamshirsaz

RISING STARS

Miss Bun

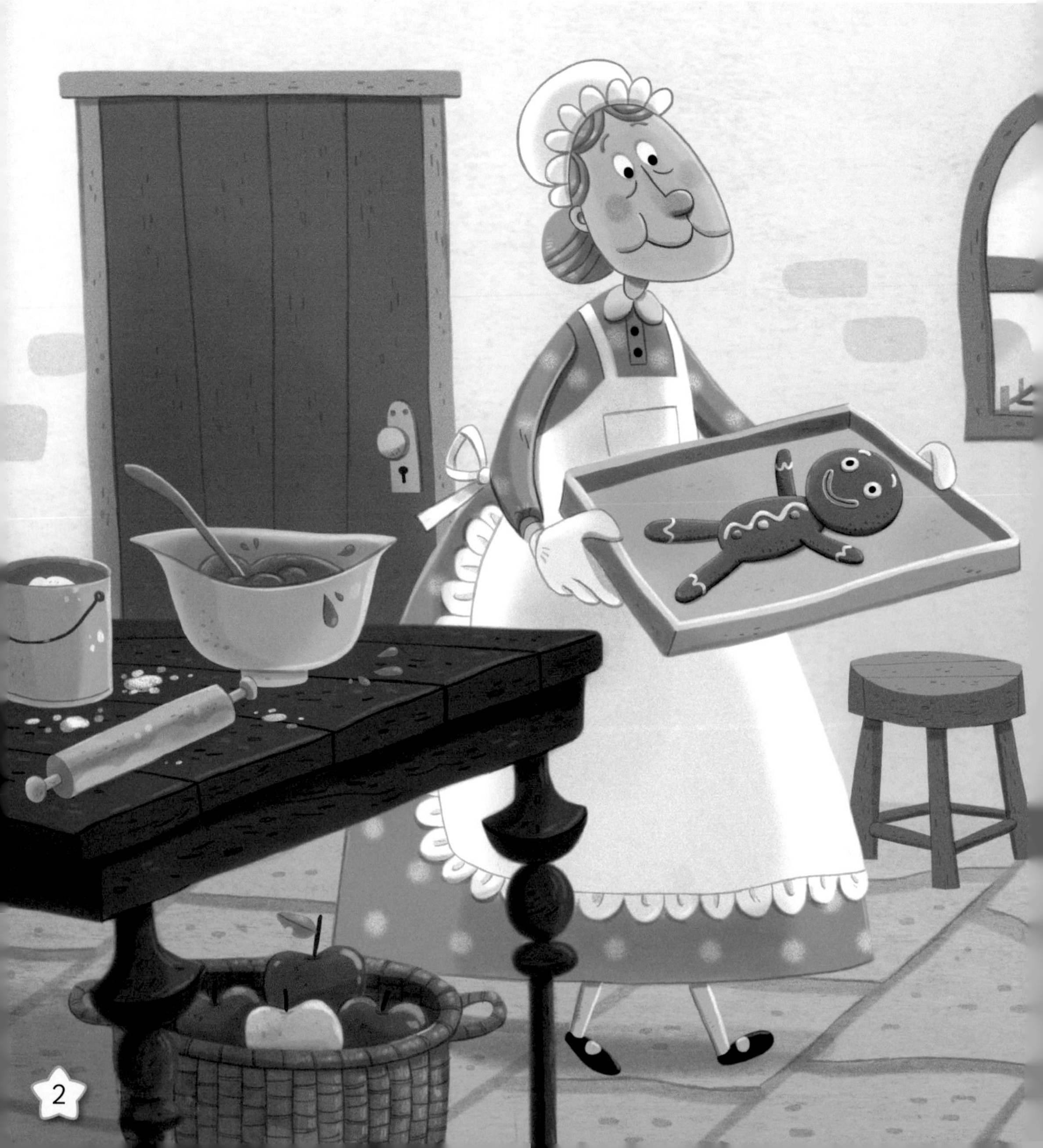

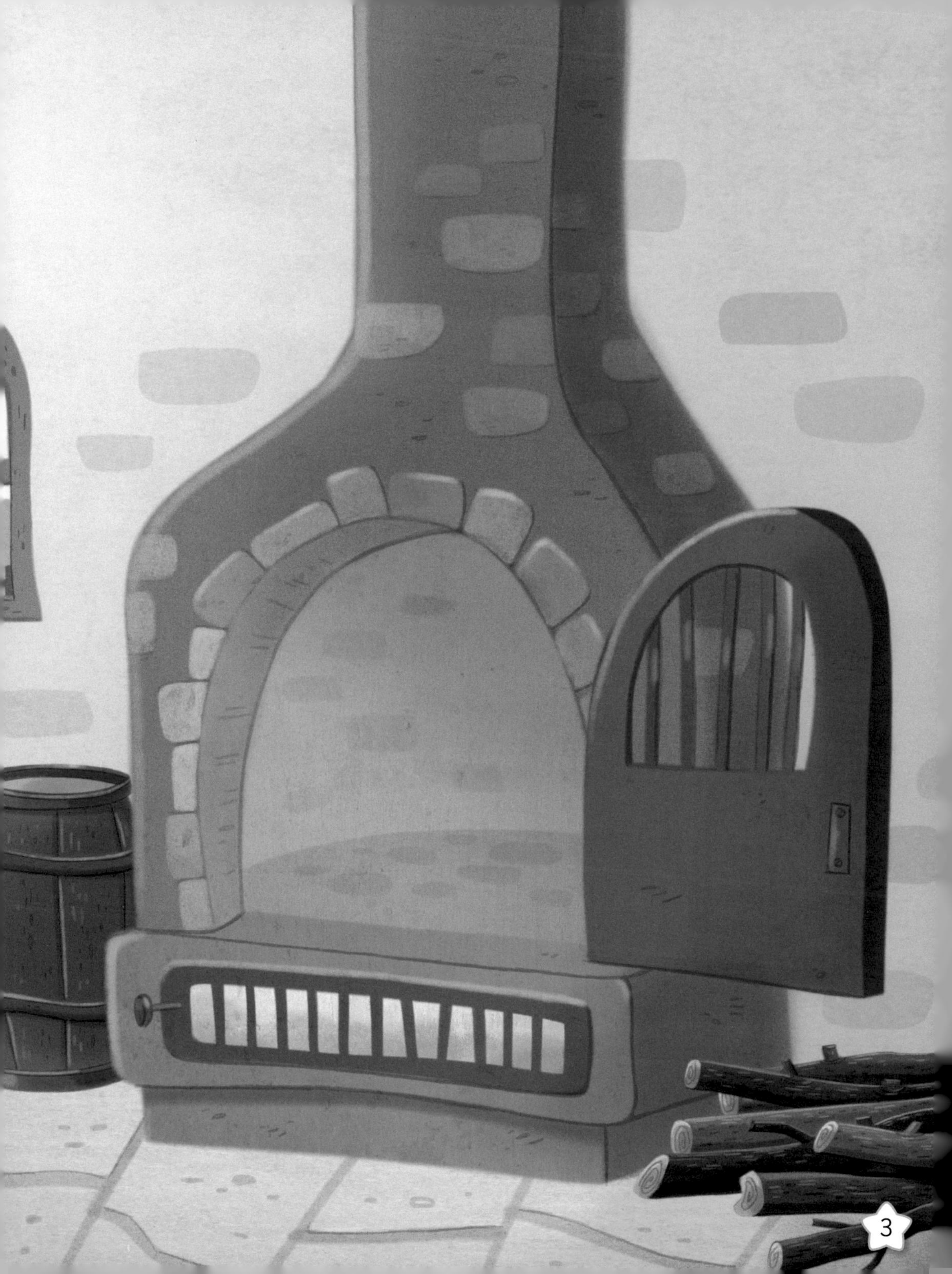

run

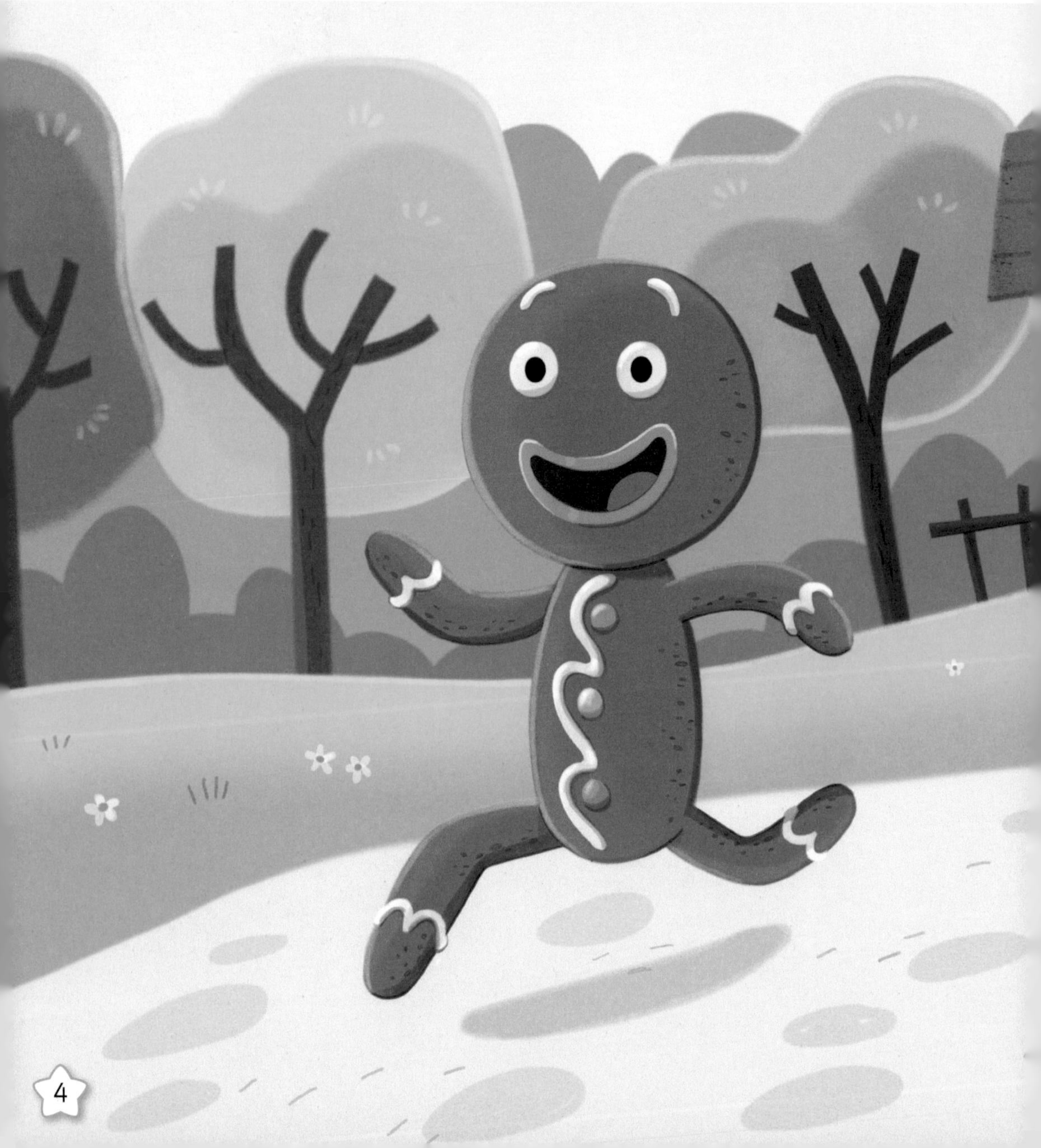

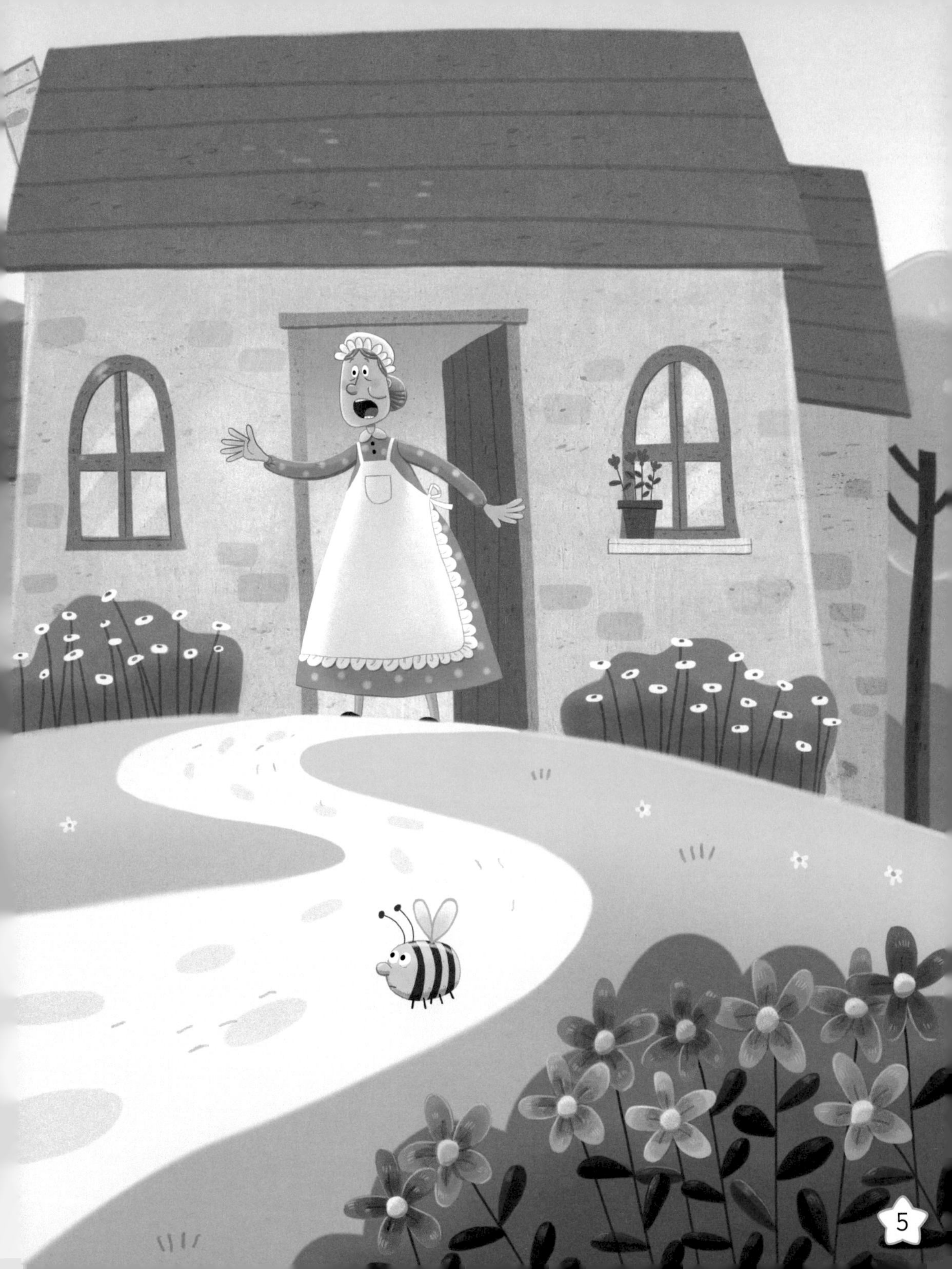

met

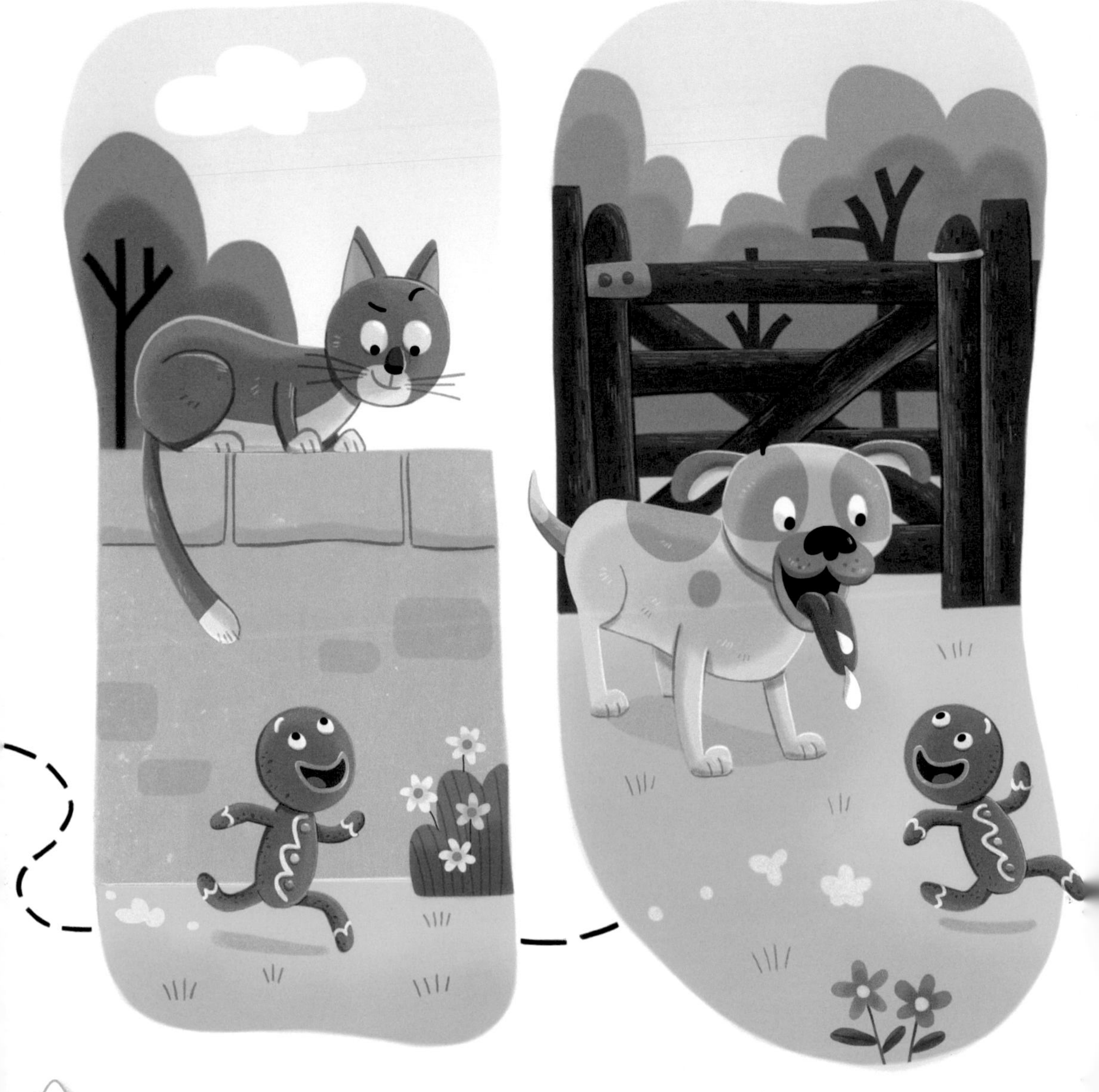

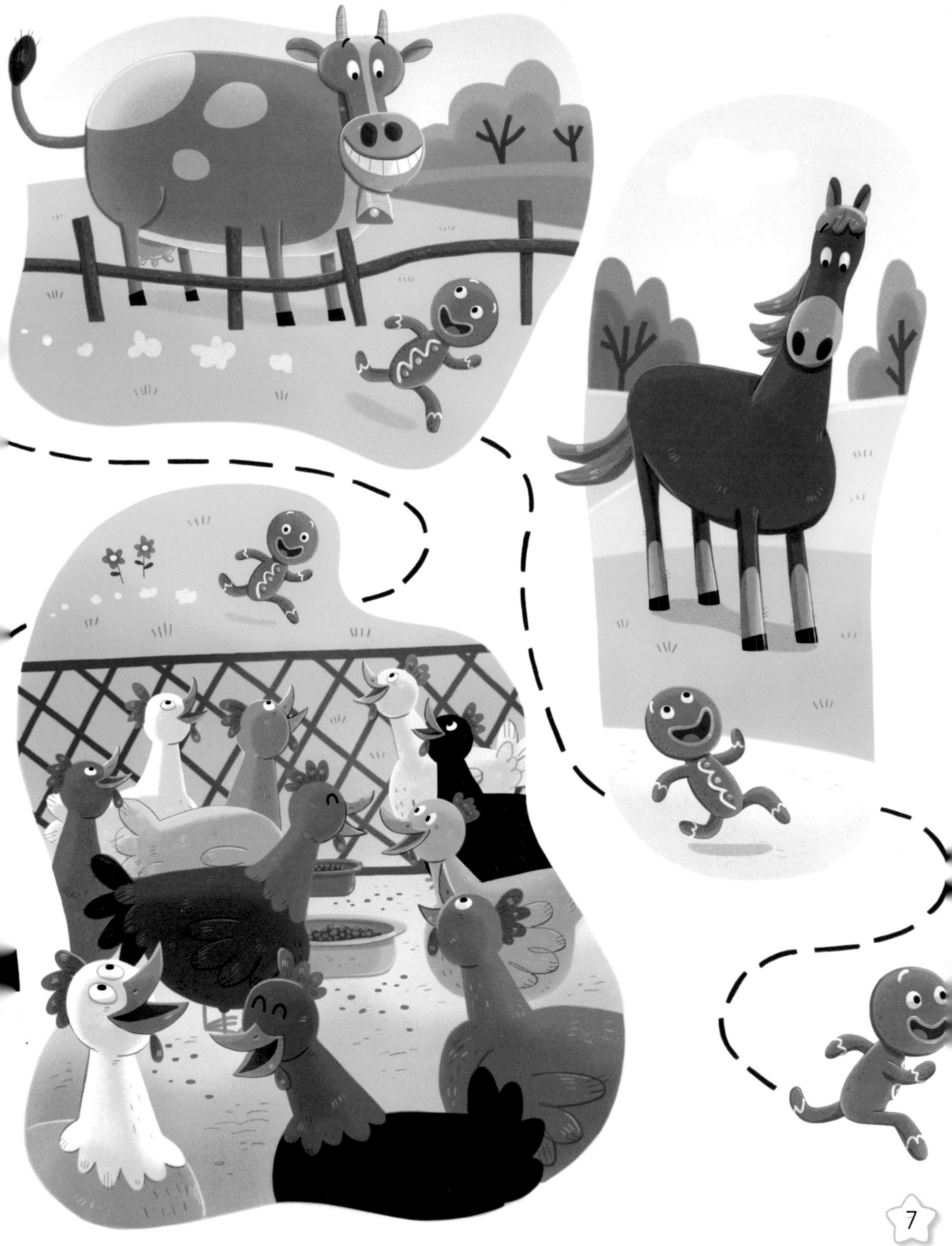

hop on

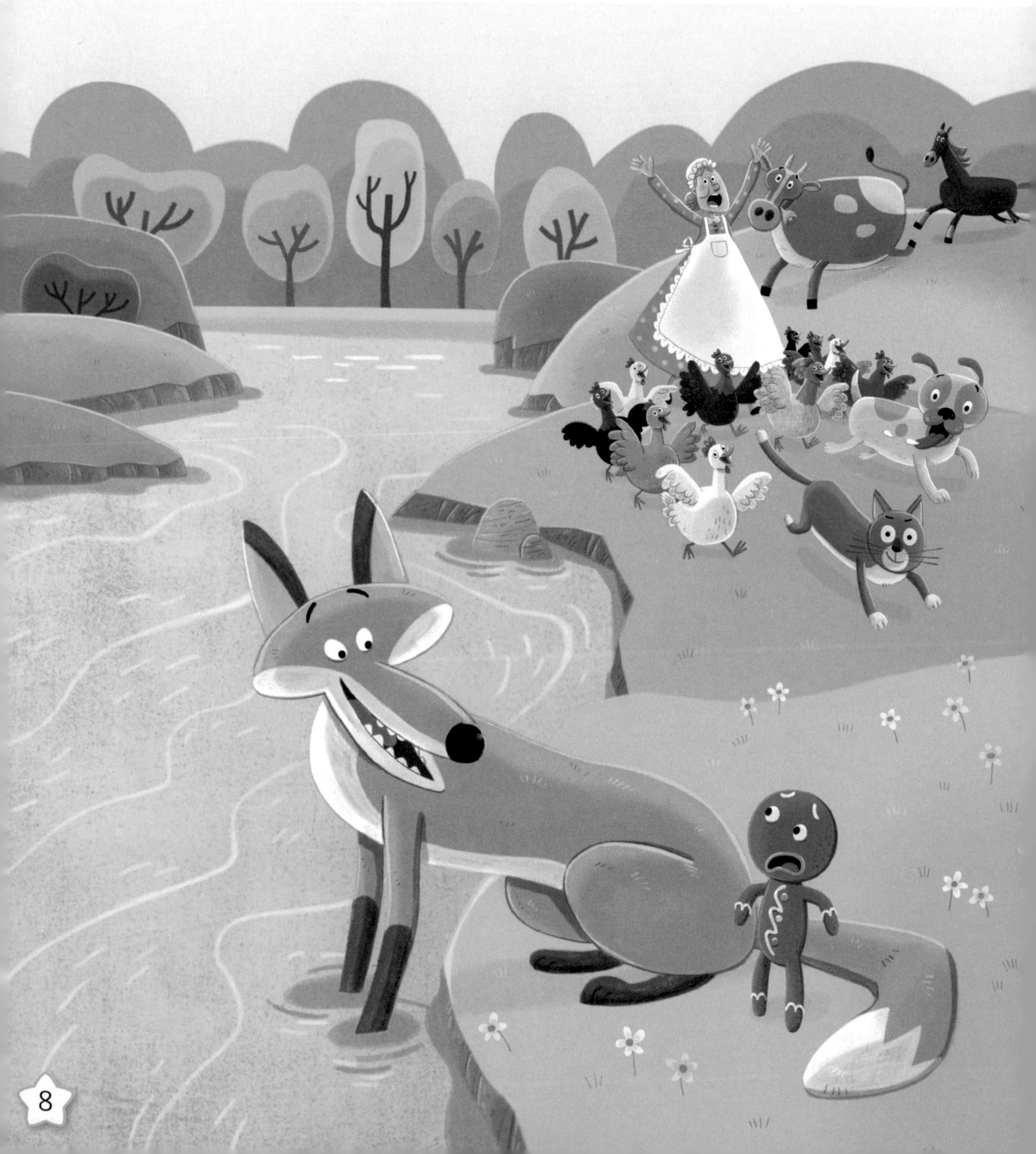